In memory of my father, Arnold Sommerfeldt, who taught me the definition of adventure. To my husband, Greg, my partner in this adventure, and to my two sons, whose adventures I will never get tired of hearing about.

Remember, Bed Bugs Have to Eat Too!

JENGA® & ©2020 Hasbro, Inc. Used with permission.
BED BUGS® & ©2020 Hasbro, Inc. Used with permission.

Library of Congress Control Number: 2020907240

CPSIA Code: PRT0820A
ISBN-13: 978-1-64307-435-1

Printed in the United States

REMEMBER

BED BUGS HAVE TO EAT TOO!

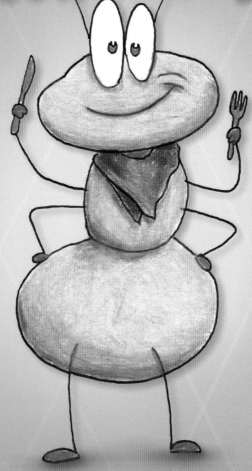

JULIEANN WORTHEN

ILLUSTRATED BY JIM CHRISTENSON

The parents tucked their boys into bed that night. "Sleep tight," they said. "Don't let the bed bugs bite!"

And with that they left, turning out the light.

Why would bed bugs bite? the boys thought,
with more than a little fright.

There was a noise in the dark—it was squeaky and small.
The boys didn't like it, not one bit at all!

They flipped on the lamp
and cried, "Who's there?"
And what they saw—
well, they couldn't help but stare.

A little, round bug called out from below,
"Hello! Have any ice cream, or maybe some Jell-O?

We are quite hungry, as perhaps you can see.
Could you help us? Pretty please?"

The bed bugs did not think of these children as prey.
They just wanted snacks to keep hunger at bay!

The boys decided that they could pitch in,
and agreed to take a trip to the kitchen.

There the fun began to unfold.
The bed bugs and boys found snacks that were like gold.

Cookies, marshmallows, ice cream, and white cake!
Veggies, hot chocolate, soup with crackers, leftover T-bone steak.

Once they had enough to eat, and they put away the toaster, where was the party? Well, let's just say it wasn't over.

They formed a parade to the table,
carrying extra snacks and drinks of all sorts.
What's next? Games, of course!

The bed bugs brought
out the cards and the dice,
and the boys brought
their favorite handheld gaming device.

"Oh no!" said the bed bugs.
"They don't make those that small.
If you play with us,
you can't use those at all."

So the boys put them away and opened the closet door where they had been just moments before.

They rummaged around and soon found a favorite classic, the Bed Bugs game. It was a hoot! The bugs jumped around like magic!

After some time, the bugs pulled out the dice and the cards,

and the boys thought, "Wow! They are diehards."

They played 'til the wee hours,
laughing when toppling Jenga towers.

As playtime wound down for the night, one tired boy had an idea.
He was quite bright!

"How about the laptop? It can be a bed bug movie screen!"
Impressed, the bugs said, "For US? It's as big as we've ever seen!"

Fifty tiny bed bugs felt quite cushy,
as they nestled together all mushy, squooshy.

"Look at the time! Whoops, we better get to bed just like our mom and dad said!"

The boys crawled into bed and fell asleep,
and it seemed only seconds had passed
when the alarm began to beep.

After a full day,
the next night came around.
The boys were looking forward
to seeing the friends they had found.

The parents dutifully tucked
the boys in again at night,
"Good night. Sleep tight.
Don't let the bed bugs bite!"

The boys laughed out loud
and said what is true:
"But mom and dad,
bed bugs have to eat too!"

So next time someone says,
"Good night! Sleep tight!
Don't let the bed bugs bite!"

You'll know just what to do.
Smile and say,

"REMEMBER, BED BUGS HAVE TO EAT TOO!"

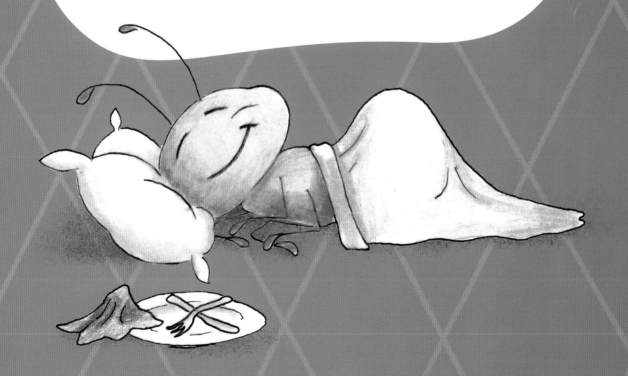

ABOUT THE AUTHOR

JulieAnn Worthen believes life is a beautiful, grand adventure. As a graduate of EIU, SIUE, and UMKC, JulieAnn has studied and enjoyed literature and writing for years. She is a proud wife, mother, and (appropriately) the fearless leader of the Adventure Club, a travel club in Minnesota. She is grateful to have grown up in a home filled with laughter, and credits her father, the true inspiration for writing *Remember, Bed Bugs Have to Eat Too!* One night while tucking her son in with the ritualistic phrase she was raised on, "Good night! Sleep tight! Don't let the bed bugs bite!" JulieAnn's father—who was listening in on speakerphone— interjected, "Good night! But remember, those poor bed bugs have to eat too!" This was a typical thing for her dad to say, but it sparked the idea for the playful children's book brought to life in these pages by a fantastic illustrator who captured the family's zany sense of humor!

Happy adventuring through this book, and through all of your life's many adventures!

ABOUT THE ILLUSTRATOR

Illustrator Jim Christenson can't remember a time when he was without a pencil, pen, brush, or lump of clay. When he was three years old, he constructed a three-dimensional paper replica of his brother's graduation cap, tassel included. His parents were so impressed, they topped his brother's cake with it. From that moment on, Jim has been creating artwork for the enjoyment of others. Around the age of twelve, Jim started to pursue the craft seriously by taking art lessons online and from a professional artist, whose realism, attention to detail, skill, and knowledge he admired, respected, and coveted. These experiences influenced his experimentation with different mediums including wood, rice paper, clay, pastels, stained glass, mosaics, colored pencil, gouache, and others. He studied animation and cartooning with a Disney animator who helped him develop an entire animated film, giving him a deeper appreciation for the classic, hand-drawn Disney movies. Each of these experiences helped Jim hone his passion for illustration. He enjoyed imagining and creating the entertaining mischief that two boys and a host of friendly bed bugs would engage in during the night, and he hopes you thoroughly enjoy *Remember, Bed Bugs Have to Eat Too!*